71/4.95

10-11-00

NJV P+T

YOU GOTTA TRY THIS!

MORE SCIENCE FUN
by VICKI COBB and KATHY DARLING

Bet You Can!
Science Possibilities to Fool You

Bet You Can't
Science Impossibilities to Fool You

Don't Try This at Home!
Science Fun for Kids on the Go

Wanna Bet?
Science Challenges to Fool You

YOU GOTTA TRY THIS!

Absolutely Irresistible Science

VICKI COBB and KATHY DARLING

Illustrated by TRUE KELLEY

Morrow Junior Books
New York

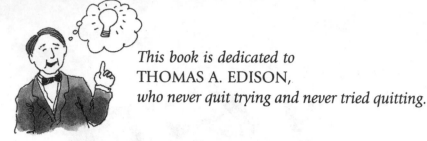

This book is dedicated to
THOMAS A. EDISON,
who never quit trying and never tried quitting.

PLEASE NOTE THAT SOME OF
THE EXPERIMENTS IN THIS
BOOK ARE TO BE PERFORMED
UNDER ADULT SUPERVISION.

Published by Morrow Junior Books
a division of William Morrow and Company, Inc.
1350 Avenue of the Americas, New York, NY 10019
www.williammorrow.com

Printed in the United States of America.

10   9   8   7   6   5   4   3   2

Library of Congress Cataloging-in-Publication Data
Cobb, Vicki.
You gotta try this!: absolutely irresistible science / by Vicki Cobb and Kathy
Darling; illustrated by True Kelley.
p. cm.
Includes index.
Summary: A collection of science experiments and activities, arranged in
such categories as "Physical Attractions," "Curious Chemistry," and "Freaky
Fluids."
ISBN 0-688-15740-8
1. Science—Experiments—Juvenile literature.   2. Scientific recreations—
Juvenile literature.   [1. Science—Experiments.   2. Experiments.
3. Scientific recreations.]   I. Darling, Kathy.   II. Kelley, True, ill.   III. Title.
Q164.C538 1999   507.8—dc21   98-29556   CIP AC

CONTENTS

Don't Take Our Word For It

The amazing scientific oddities and weird observations in this book will blow you away. Would you believe that you can make your lips lie to you? That you can set a speed record for unrolling toilet paper? Or that it's possible to give artificial respiration to a fly? And how about making fireworks from a grape or a saw from kitchen cleanser? These things sound outrageous, and they are. They are also true.

How do we know? We did each trick. (We also tried many more that didn't work. Flops and bombs didn't make the cut.)

Science is a way of knowing by trying. So don't take our word for it. It's not in the spirit of science to believe what you read or what someone tells you. Nothing beats doing it yourself—except maybe sharing it.

While we were researching this book, friends, family, even the mail carrier looked forward to hearing us yell, "You gotta try this!" Now it's your turn. You gotta try it and see for yourself. Ready, set, go to it!

GETTING PERSONAL 1

Just because you live in your body doesn't mean that you know it all that well. You can fool it and it can fool you. Your senses do the best they can, but often that's just not good enough. They have some weak points you probably never noticed. Not to worry, though. Little known facts about touch, taste, sight, and hearing are great opportunities for experimenting on yourself and your friends.

Welcome to science—up close and personal.

STRETCHING THE TRUTH

Make your lips lie to you.

This experiment is not for people who care about keeping up appearances. You're going to have to stretch your face out of shape.

> You will need:
> - a piece of stiff cardboard (A business card is about the right size.)
> - a friend

Lips are very touch sensitive. Test this out and see for yourself. Close your eyes and mouth. Have a friend gently press the corner of a card between your lips. The card should be held vertically so that its edges press against the upper and lower lip at the same time. Try to determine whether the card is straight up and down or tilted right or left at an angle. Chances are you'll get it right every time.

Now fix it so your lips will lie. Put your right index finger on the skin above your upper lip and pull right. Put your left index finger on the skin under your lower lip and pull left. Again close your eyes. Now have your friend insert the corner of the card between your lips as before. This time, even when the card is straight up and down, it will feel as if it's slanted.

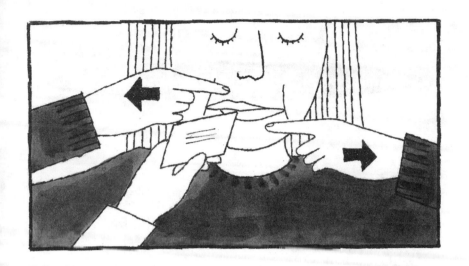

Insider Information

When the card touches your lips, the pressure triggers nerves. The brain knows where those nerves are located because you have a lifetime of receiving messages from lined-up lips. But pull them out of alignment, and the brain is fooled. In the absence of sight, the message from your twisted lips is interpreted by your brain to mean that the card isn't straight.

Can the brain learn to adjust to twisted lips and interpret things correctly again? Yes, but it takes time. Scientists had a man wear prism eyeglasses all the time so that everything he saw was upside down. After three weeks of living like this, he woke up one day and everything appeared right side up. His brain had adjusted. When he took off the glasses, everything was upside down again. Fortunately, the effect wasn't permanent.

WEiGH COOL

Cold cash is heavier than you think. You can increase the weight of a coin by chilling it in the freezer . . . but there's a catch. You must use your fingertips as a scale.

> You will need:
> - a blindfolded friend
> - 2 quarters
> - a freezer or ice cubes
> - a towel

O rdinarily, the pressure receptors in the fingertips are pretty accurate at measuring weight. Use a blindfolded friend as your human scale. Have the "weigher" face you with hands palm up and the middle and index fingers extended. Place a quarter on the fingertips of each hand. Ask your "scale" to compare the weights. The hands may be moved up and down to help make the evaluation.

Put one of the coins against an ice cube or in the freezer for several minutes. Dry it off with a towel and repeat the test. Surprisingly, the cold coin will feel substantially heavier.

Insider Information

Why a cold object feels heavier than one at room temperature is a mystery. One possible explanation is that the nerves responsible for pressure (weight) are also triggered by cold. Does a hot coin feel lighter than one at room temperature? We experimented and couldn't detect any difference. But check it out for yourself. Maybe your nerves aren't as frayed as ours.

AN ANTISTRETCHING WORKOUT

Painlessly shorten your arm.

Most workouts are designed to lengthen and stretch the muscles and tendons of your body. This is an exercise that does just the opposite. Or so it appears.

You will need:
• a wall

Face a wall and position yourself so that the fingertips of an extended arm just touch it.

Keep your arm straight, and in a single motion swing it down and behind you, then back up to its original position. Your fingers are now unable to make contact with the wall. Honey, I shrunk your arm!

Insider Information

Relax. Your arm has not really shrunk. When you swing it behind you, you unconsciously lean backward. For some unknown reason, your body does not return to its original position when you swing your arm forward again.

Now try the exercise again. Even though you know what happened before and why, it doesn't matter. You'll get the same "short arm." You can't override your unconscious sense of balance.

UNWANTED ADVANCES

Normally, you would have no difficulty jogging in place. However, you can fix it so that you can't. No matter how you try to restrain yourself, you will move forward.

You will need:
- a treadmill
- a blindfold
- a friend

Begin by jogging on a level treadmill. Hold on as a friend blindfolds you. Continue jogging for several minutes while still holding on. Have your friend turn off the machine. Then have him or her help you off the treadmill and face you toward a clear pathway. Do not remove the blindfold.

Try jogging in place. You will move forward although you will feel as if you are a superstationary jogger.

Insider Information

Although it may seem like it, jogging on a treadmill is not jogging in place. You are moving forward. You don't go anywhere because the floor of the treadmill is moving backward at the same rate.

Nerves tell your muscles how to move. A repetitive movement such as jogging causes nerves in use to become fatigued. They continue to fire in the same pattern when the repetitive action is suddenly stopped. So, when you're on solid ground, you continue to move forward as you did on the treadmill. When you remove your blindfold, vision takes over, and you can make the adjustments that allow you to jog in place.

Now try hopping on the treadmill. After you get off, try to hop in place with the same leg you used on the treadmill. Once again, you will move forward. However, if you use the other leg, you will be able to hop in place.

BAD TASTE GENES

Use orange juice to see if you've inherited a sensitivity to bitter taste.

You may be able to change the way orange juice tastes just by brushing your teeth.

> You will need:
> - toothpaste containing sodium lauryl sulfate
> - a toothbrush
> - a small glass of orange juice

First take a sip of orange juice and notice its flavor. Rinse your mouth with water. Brush your teeth for at least sixty seconds with a toothpaste containing sodium lauryl sulfate. Rinse with water and taste the juice again. Does it have a different flavor?

One out of three people does not detect any difference. The others do. And it's mouth puckering. Yuck!

Insider Information

The tongue is equipped with taste buds that can detect four basic tastes: sweet, salty, sour, and bitter. Sodium lauryl sulfate is a detergent often found in toothpaste, mouthwash, and laundry products. This harmless chemical can alter the taste of the citric acid in orange juice. The sourness is almost unchanged, but the bitterness is almost ten times stronger.

Your ability to taste bitterness in other substances is inherited as well. If both of your parents gave you the bitterness-detecting gene, then caffeine, the food preservative sodium benzoate, tonic water, and certain artificial sweeteners have an especially bitter flavor. If only one parent gave you the gene, you can detect a bitter taste, but it won't be unpleasant. If you didn't get the gene, you might not be able to identify bitterness at all.

SPOOKY SURVEILLANCE

Try to escape the watching eyes of a mask.

A stationary mask can appear to follow your every movement. No matter what direction you move, the mask seems to turn with you.

You will need:
- a molded mask (We used a Halloween hockey mask.)
- tape
- a sunlit window

 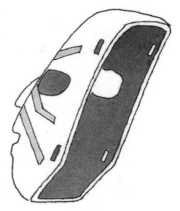

This illusion depends on using a mask that is molded so that the inside surface is the exact opposite of the outside. (The inside surfaces of some masks are smooth. These won't work.) The mask must also be translucent. (Some light has to be able to pass through it.) It doesn't matter if the mask is painted on the outside.

Mask taped to a sunny window

10 feet

To experience this illusion, tape the mask onto a sunlit window. The molded outside should be against the pane, and the hollow inside should be facing the room. The sun must be shining directly into the window because the mask has to be lit from behind.

Stand ten or more feet away from the mask. Position yourself so that you are facing the window and the mask is on your left side. Stand still and focus on the mask. It will no longer appear hollow; it will look as if you are viewing the outer side. If you have trouble seeing the illusion, try closing one eye. Watch the mask as you walk past it, moving parallel to the window. The effect is startling. You can't get away from the mask's spooky surveillance.

Insider Information

The mask seems to be tracking you for two reasons, neither of which is supernatural. First, the back-lighting removes some of your ability to judge depth. Your brain doesn't have enough information to tell whether you are viewing the hollow inside of the mask or the convex outer side. Since you're more familiar with a bulging face, your brain goes with the more "normal" perception.

Not only can you be tricked by backlighting as to the shape of the mask, but you can be fooled by motion as well. If you tape a mask to a window with the normal side facing the room, the eyes and face appear to turn away from you as you walk past. When you walk by a mask with the hollow side facing the room, everything is reversed, including the direction the face appears to turn.

The Haunted Mansion in Disney World makes good use of this chilling illusion. Instead of a mask, hollow statues with lights inside them stare at you as you ride by.

WHIPPING UP AN ILLUSION

Stop a whirling eggbeater with your TV.

Whirl an eggbeater. You know it's moving because you're turning the handle. Besides, you can see the blades rotating. You can, however, make them appear to stop.

> You will need:
> - a hand rotary eggbeater
> - a TV or computer screen

Holding the eggbeater at eye level, point it at a TV or computer screen and turn the handle. Look at the screen through the spinning blades.

Experiment with the speed of the whirling blades and see what happens. At thirty revolutions per second, the blades will appear motionless. Speed up and they'll start moving again. Slow down and the blades will appear to reverse direction. Go ahead—beat your brains out.

Insider Information

You've beaten your brains because you've tricked them. The stopping and reversing of the blades is an illusion.

When you look at a whirling eggbeater, the blades appear to be a blur. They're moving too fast for you to see the individual blades. When you look at the spinning blades against the background of a TV or computer screen, separate images of the blades start to appear. Although the light of the screen appears to be a steady light, it is flashing, and you get images of the blades only when the light flashes.

If the speed of the blades is the same as the speed of the flashing light (thirty times per second), a blade reaches the same place every flash, causing the blades to appear motionless. This stop-motion illusion is called a *stroboscopic effect*. Spin until you establish the stop-motion speed. Slow down slightly and the blades will appear to reverse direction. When you spin faster than the stop-motion speed, they appear to be moving forward.

Rotating car hubcaps can also show the stroboscopic effect when they are viewed under certain kinds of street lamps. Like TV or computer screens, highway lights flicker. To get the stop-motion illusion, you must be traveling at night on a highway lit by yellow or pink mercury or sodium vapor lights. Look at the hubcaps of cars traveling beside you. The holes in the hubcap will appear stationary at about sixty miles per hour.

CENTS OF HEARING

Sort pennies by sound.

There's no challenge to sorting pennies by the year they were made if you look at the date stamped on them. It's harder, but still possible, to sort old pennies from new ones by sound.

You will need:
- an assortment of pennies, old and new
- a bathroom or kitchen with a tile floor
- a friend

Divide the pennies into two piles, one consisting of coins minted in 1982 and earlier, and the other of coins made in 1983 or later. So far your sorting has been done by sight. Now you're ready to test your ability to sort by sound!

Close your eyes so that you can concentrate all your attention on listening. Have your friend hold the new pennies in one hand and the old ones in the other. Your assistant should drop them one by one in a random pattern from each group onto a tile floor. Your assistant should identify which pile each coin came from after you've heard the sound. Soon you will be able to hear a difference and tell the new pennies from the old by sound alone. Practice by calling out "old" or "new" with confirmation from your assistant.

Insider Information

One-cent coins were once called coppers, because they were made of copper. But the price of this metal rose faster than the value of a penny. To cut costs, the U.S. government decided to make pennies out of a cheaper metal, zinc, and plate them with copper. Zinc pennies were first mass produced in 1983. They look the same as the coppers, but they don't sound the same. Newer pennies make a dull, tinny noise when dropped. Older ones make a sharper, ringing sound.

A BiG YAWN

Prove yawns are contagious.

People usually yawn when they're sleepy or bored. But you can make a normal well-rested person yawn just by looking at you. In fact, you can start a yawn epidemic.

> You will need:
> - people or animals

Make eye contact with someone as you noisily open your mouth in a gigantic yawn. You don't have to show your tonsils—a covered-mouth yawn is just as contagious. Don't worry if you're a bad actor: A faked yawn usually turns into the real thing. In fact, you may be yawning right now.

The odds are very high that your victim will not be able to resist. In a room full of people, the yawn

will spread rapidly, even to those who don't see yawners. Sound alone can spread a yawn.

Insider Information

Yawning is not just for the tired or bored. People will do this when they are trying to pay attention in a difficult situation or when they are nervous. But in spite of scientific research, we still do not know exactly why we yawn. The most popular theory is that there is a lack of oxygen in the brain. Yawning is a fast way of taking in a lot of oxygen in one breath. After all, the mouth is bigger than the nose.

While we don't know why we yawn, we do know what happens during one. Look closely at a yawning person. The pupils expand, the muscles in the forehead tighten, and the lips push against the teeth.

Yawns can even be spread from one species to another. Watching your dog or cat yawn can make you do the same thing. Interestingly, cats seem to be immune to human yawning. Yawn in front of your dog, though, and, sooner or later, it will yawn back.

Research has shown that yawning is most infectious among strangers. Kathy doesn't know if this is entirely true. Vicki certainly makes her yawn.

Yawning isn't the only contagious activity. Scratching is also transmitted by the "power of suggestion."

PHYSICAL ATTRACTIONS

The world has been transformed by the science of physics. Before we understood forces—motion, heat, sound, magnetism, electricity—people lived a low-tech life. Even though playing with low-tech stuff has gone on for thousands of years, it can still surprise you.

On the other hand, high-tech innovations continually amaze us. You may have to be a "rocket scientist" to invent some of these machines, but you don't have to be one to find new uses for TVs or computers. You're in the right place to discover the power of physical attractions.

STOP THE DROP

Use paper clips to prevent keys from hitting the floor.

A ring of keys is clearly heavier than three paper clips. But the three clips can counterbalance the keys and stop their fall.

You will need:
- keys on a key ring
- a piece of string about one yard long
- 3 paper clips
- a pen or pencil

Tie the keys to one end of a piece of string and the paper clips to the other end.

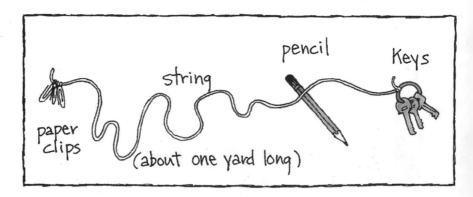

$\frac{2}{3}$ of the string is held horizontally.

And $\frac{1}{3}$ of the string hangs down.

Hold a pencil horizontally in front of you with one hand. Grasp the paper clips in the other. Drape the string over the pencil so the keys are hanging down.

Make the string between the pencil and the clips horizontal. Two-thirds of the string should be between the clips and the pencil.

Now let go of the paper clips. Naturally, the keys drop. But amazingly, they don't reach the ground. The paper clips spin around the pencil and wind up the string. Six wraps are enough to break the fall of the keys.

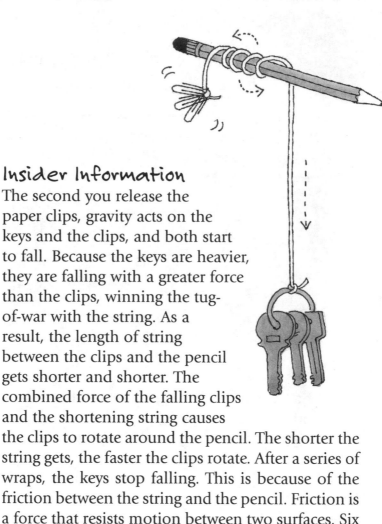

Insider Information

The second you release the paper clips, gravity acts on the keys and the clips, and both start to fall. Because the keys are heavier, they are falling with a greater force than the clips, winning the tug-of-war with the string. As a result, the length of string between the clips and the pencil gets shorter and shorter. The combined force of the falling clips and the shortening string causes the clips to rotate around the pencil. The shorter the string gets, the faster the clips rotate. After a series of wraps, the keys stop falling. This is because of the friction between the string and the pencil. Friction is a force that resists motion between two surfaces. Six wraps usually provide enough friction to stop the fall of several keys.

AN ALARM CUP

Use a paper cup to make a VERY loud roar.

Believe it or not, a paper cup and dental floss can blast everyone out of bed.

You will need:
- a paper cup
- a wooden toothpick
- a twenty-four-inch length of waxed dental floss, preferably the ribbon kind

24 inches long

Dental Floss

With the toothpick, punch a small hole in the center of the bottom of a paper cup.

Thread the dental floss through the hole and tie this end around a broken-off piece of the toothpick. This will keep the floss from slipping back through the hole.

Hold the cup in one hand and grasp the dental floss between your thumb and index finger. Gently pull your fingers along the string. The sound speaks volumes!

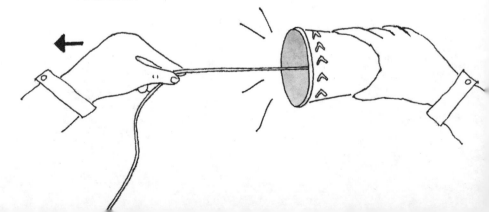

Insider Information

Your roaring cup creates sound the same way a violin does. As your fingers move along the dental floss, the sticky wax turns the stroke into a lot of tiny stops and starts. This causes the string to vibrate. Rosin on a bow does the same thing to a violin's string. The cup amplifies the vibrations.

Your paper cup is not a one-note instrument. Tie the loose end of the floss to a stationary object. Pull the cup so the thread is tight and then run your fingers down the string; the tighter the string the higher the sound. Now try plucking the string.

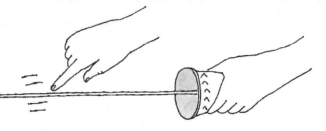

Dental floss music has never really become popular. Aside from the fact that this instrument makes a terrible sound, there's another drawback. The string has to be replaced when the wax becomes smooth.

THE FiFTY-FiVE-CENT FiX

Do a coin-flip trick you can't lose.

When you drop a coin, you have a fifty-fifty chance of getting heads. When you drop a pair of coins, you can stack them in a way that also stacks the odds. The coin that starts out on top ends up on the bottom 100 percent of the time. You can't lose!

You will need:
- 2 quarters
- a nickel

Make a sandwich of the coins with the nickel in the middle. Hold the stack between your thumb and index finger so the coins are horizontal.

 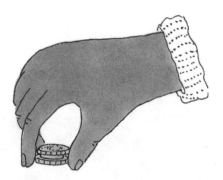

Cup your other hand about ten inches below the coins. Spread your fingertips apart so you release the bottom quarter yet still hold on to the top one. The quarter starts its downward trip with the nickel riding on top. Surprisingly, when the two coins land in your hand, the quarter is on top.

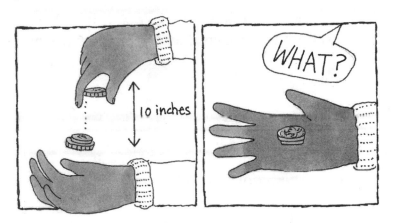

Insider Information

Why does the nickel always end up below the quarter? The coins flip. Holding on to the top quarter makes it nearly impossible to release both sides of the bottom quarter at the same instant, so one side drops sooner, causing both coins to rotate. It takes a fall of about ten inches for the nickel and the quarter to flip over (turn 180 degrees).

If the coins flip 180 degrees in a ten-inch drop, how far would they have to travel to make a 360-degree rotation so the nickel is back on top? You might think twenty inches. But gravity is working here, causing the coins to accelerate as they fall. It would take a forty-inch drop to accomplish this feat.

A CANDLE TAKES A BATH

Burn a candle under water.

Light a candle in a bowl of water, and it will continue to burn even when the wick is below the surface of the water, creating the oddest-shaped candle
you've ever seen.

You will need:
- a six-inch candle
- a short candleholder with a spike or
  waterproof tape (adhesive or duct tape)
- matches
- a glass bowl
- scissors
- cold water

CAUTION: THIS TRICK INVOLVES FIRE, SO
GET AN ADULT ASSISTANT TO HELP YOU.

The hardest part of the setup is attaching the
candle to the bottom of the bowl so that it
doesn't float when you add water. If you can't find a
short candleholder with a spike, light the candle and
drip melted wax into the center of the bowl before
adding water. Make a puddle of wax that is wider
than the candle. Quickly stick the candle into it. Let

the wax cool and harden. Secure the wax to the bowl with waterproof tape for extra holding power.

Fill the bowl with cold water up to the rim of the candle. Straighten the wick. Light it and wait.

Insider Information

A very thin wall of wax remains standing as the candle burns, preventing the water from extinguishing the flame. The water draws so much heat from the wax that the outer layer never gets hot enough to burn. If you wait long enough, your submarine candle will become a thin, hollow tube. Bet your friends won't be able to figure out how you made it.

DOUBLE RINGER

Make a bell ring with two different sounds.

You might think a bell can ring with only one sound. Not true! You can get it to make two sounds at the same time. One is the familiar ring produced by a clapper hitting the side of the bell. You can add a second sound with a piece of wood.

You will need:
- a large handheld metal bell
- a smooth wooden stick, such as the handle of a tool or a wooden spoon

With your less-favored hand, grasp the bell by the handle, making sure that you are not touching the bell itself. The bell should be facing down. Hold a piece of wood in your other hand. Press the wood against the lower rim of the bell and move it repeatedly around the circumference with a smooth, circular motion. The bell should start to hum softly and get louder and louder. If it doesn't, check to make sure that you are keeping the wood in contact with the bell and that your hands aren't.

Once you've built up a vibrating hum, move the stick away and gently ring the bell normally. Listen for the two distinct sounds coming from it.

(1.) Hold the bell facing down.

Press the wood against the bell rim.

(2.) Rub the wood around the bell rim.

(3.) Ring the bell.

RING! HUM!!

Insider Information

A bell rings because metal vibrates a long time after it is struck. (You can eliminate the ring by holding the bell rather than the handle. If your hand prevents the metal from vibrating, the bell makes only a short clunky sound as the clapper hits the side.) The vibrations in your double-sounding bell are created in two ways: by a single sharp hit and by many small ones. The bang of the clapper is obviously a sharp hit. What you might not realize is that wood stroked along the rim creates many small hits. The wood appears to be moving smoothly around the lip, but it's not. It is slipping and stopping many times per second. (Another demonstration of this kind of sound generation is the ring of a crystal glass caused by running a wet finger around the rim.)

The double ringer has two tones because the impact sound of the clapper is different from the ringing tone.

WHERE'S THE RUB?

Feel invisible ridges on a refrigerator magnet.

Common flexible magnets (the kind with advertising on them) have a secret. They look and feel smooth. However, they have a hidden roughness. You can't see it, but you can feel it.

> You will need:
> - a flat rubber or plastic refrigerator magnet
> - scissors
> - a piece of white paper (optional)
> - iron filings (optional)

Cut a flat rubber magnet in half. Press the unprinted sides together. Depending on which way you put them together, one of three things can happen: The pieces don't stick together, they stick weakly, or they stick strongly.

You won't be able to detect the hidden roughness of the magnet if the sides don't stick together. So rotate one piece ninety degrees. It will stick either strongly or weakly to the other piece. In each case, though, when you rub the pieces back and forth against each other, they will feel as if they have ridges.

Insider Information

A magnet is made from a material that can attract pieces of iron and other magnetic materials. If a bar-shaped magnet is suspended so that it can swing freely, it will line up with one end pointing north and the other pointing south. The end pointing north is its north pole; the end pointing south, its south pole.

Flexible magnets are not solid magnets. They are made of many rows of tiny bar magnets embedded in a rubber sheet. A row of north poles alternates with a row of south poles. The rows are about an eighth of an inch apart. You can see where the magnetic rows are if you place a piece of white paper over the magnet and sprinkle it with iron filings. The filings will form a pattern over the magnetic rows beneath the paper.

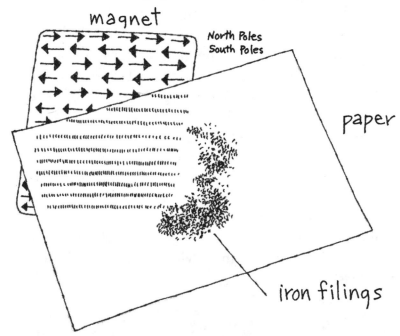

magnet

North Poles
South Poles

paper

iron filings

When the two pieces of the magnet are aligned so that the magnetic rows are parallel, you feel the corrugation as you pull them across each other. The jerky motion is caused when like poles repel each other and unlike poles attract each other. Your senses of touch and hearing interpret this as a rough surface.

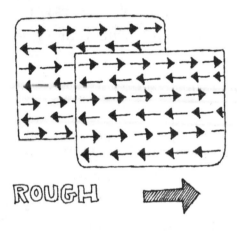

ROUGH

When the rows are at right angles, they don't line up, so the attraction is too weak to form a bond. That's why the magnets' surfaces move smoothly past each other.

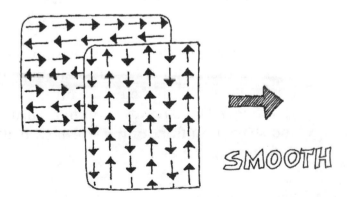

SMOOTH

REPULSIVE WRITING

Xerox and other copying machines use static electricity to write. You can, too. See the inspiration behind the dry copier with your TV set and some talcum powder.

You will need:
- a TV set
- talcum powder and a powder puff
- a dust cloth and glass cleaner or a used sheet of fabric softener

Begin with a clean, dry television screen. Turn on the TV for at least five minutes. Then turn it off. Write a simple message on the screen with your finger. Dip a powder puff into talcum powder and shake it in front of the screen so that the dust drifts toward the TV.

A thin layer of powder will coat the screen except where you wrote your message.

When you are finished, erase it by cleaning the screen with glass cleaner or a used sheet of fabric softener from the dryer.

Insider Information

Modern copying machines use a process called xerography, which means "dry writing." It is based on the principle that an electric charge will attract dust. A television screen gets a static charge when the set is on and holds the charge for a short time after it is turned off. Wherever you touch the screen, you get rid of the charge. The tiny particles of powder are attracted to the charged areas and cling there. They are repulsed wherever there is writing.

In a copying machine, dark areas of the image become electrically charged and attract particles of powdered ink. Through a complicated process, the ink is transferred to white copy paper, where it is fused to the paper with heat.

SOUND BYTES

Listen to your computer on the radio.

Your computer gives off radio waves that you can hear. It's not exactly talk radio or music to your ears, but it's interesting listening.

> You will need:
> - a computer
> - a small AM/FM radio

There are three possible sources of computer radio waves: the monitor, the hard drive, and the microprocessor.

To listen to your monitor, turn it on. Set the radio to receive AM and tune it to an area where there is no station. Turn the volume to max. Bring the radio close to the monitor. Move it away. You should hear a difference when the radio comes close to the monitor. Click the monitor on and off. The noise you hear is radio waves broadcast by your monitor.

To listen to your hard drive, place the radio close to it. Set it as you did above. Activate the drive by opening or copying a file. You should hear a change in sounds.

To listen to your processor, you'll need to switch the radio to FM. You'll also need to know the speed of your processor, because it broadcasts radio waves on that frequency. Tune to whatever frequency most closely matches your computer's speed. For example, if your processor operates at 100 MHz (megahertz), tune your dial to 100 FM. To get the most interesting broadcast, play a video game with the sound effects turned off. What you hear is computer radio at its best.

Insider Information

The Federal Communications Commission (FCC) regulates all devices that emit or receive radio waves, including computers. Look at the back of your computer and you will see its FCC identification code. There are a limited number of radio wave frequencies. The FCC assigns different frequencies to radio and television stations, shortwave radios, and cellular phone companies. This is done to ensure that you receive a signal without interference from other sources. The FCC's regulations make sure that the radio waves given off by your computer are weak and will not interfere with other incoming signals.

CURIOUS CHEMISTRY 3

This is a high-impact chapter. It's got a "bomb," an explosion, blood, and acid—all presented for your experimenting pleasure. Chemistry is the science of matter and its changes. A knowledge of those changes will enable you to do some amazing things. Curious about chemistry? Be warned: Once you get started, these chemical curiosities might not be enough.

iNSECT LiFESAVER

Give artificial respiration to a fly.

Have you ever seen a drowned fly in a glass of water or soda? It's not necessarily dead. You may be able to revive it, although most people will probably wonder why.

> You will need:
> - a drowned fly
> - salt

F ish out the unfortunate fly. Place it in a dry spot and shake some salt on it. Then wait and see what happens.

The resuscitation may be instantaneous or may take as long as fifteen minutes. After that, sign the death certificate.

Insider Information

Flies and other insects don't have lungs. They breathe through tiny air tubes called spiracles, which are located along the sides of their abdomen.

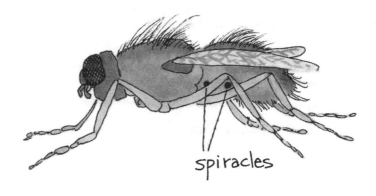

spiracles

Flies drown when their spiracles fill up with water. Salt draws the water out of the spiracles. How? First the salt dissolves in water on the surface of the insect's body. Then, because water flows to an area of higher salt content, it is drawn from the breathing spiracles.

A PLASTIC EXPLOSION

Make a sandwich-bag bomb.

This "bomb" isn't powerful, but you'll get a big bang out of it anyway!

You will need:
- a heavy-duty Ziploc sandwich bag
- water
- scissors
- a sheet of paper towel
- a measuring spoon
- baking soda
- a liquid-measuring cup
- vinegar
- a friend

Check the plastic bag for leaks by filling it with water. A leaky bag makes a dud of a bomb.

Cut or tear a paper towel into a six-inch square. Put two tablespoons of baking soda in the center of the square.

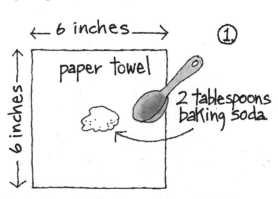

← 6 inches →   ①

paper towel

← 6 inches →

2 tablespoons baking soda

Fold one-third of the paper over the baking soda and then fold the other third over it.

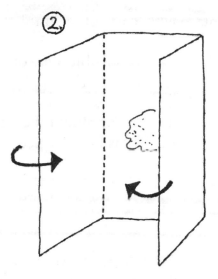

Fold the two ends up to form a packet.

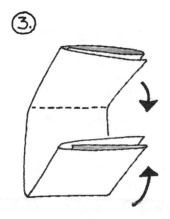

Pour a quarter cup of warm water and a half cup of vinegar in the plastic bag.

Now comes the tricky part. You have to assemble the "bomb" without letting it "explode" prematurely. This means that the vinegar and baking soda cannot come in contact with each other until the bag is completely sealed. Do this part outside or over the sink, and with a helper if possible. One of you holds the bag and starts zipping it. The other inserts the baking soda packet and holds it above the vinegar from the outside. The packet should be held above the vinegar while the bag is being sealed tightly.

$\frac{1}{4}$ cup warm water + $\frac{1}{2}$ cup vinegar

Once the bag is closed, release the packet and shake the bag. Drop the bomb in the sink or on the ground outside.

As the vinegar and baking soda mix, the bag inflates, plastic straining on all sides. Something's got to give. And it does, with a satisfying bang.

Insider Information

The destructive power of an explosion comes from expanding gases. In this case, the gas is carbon dioxide produced from a chemical reaction between baking soda and vinegar. As the gas is produced, the pressure builds inside the plastic bag. Finally the bag gives way at its weakest point—usually the Ziploc seal. The gas rushes out at a very high speed, causing an audible shock wave. *Pop!*

This bomb will not cause a fiery explosion. In fact, just the opposite. Carbon dioxide extinguishes flames. If you would like to test this for yourself, get help from an adult assistant. Have him or her light a match and lower it into the exploded bag. The flame will go out. Since carbon dioxide is heavier than air, the gas will remain there for a while, even if the bag stays open.

A GAS BOMB

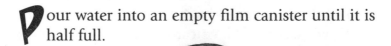

Explode a film canister.

Who would think you could make an explosion with a stomach remedy? Well, you can. Alka-Seltzer is powerful stuff. You don't even need a whole tablet. A half will do.

You will need:
- water
- a plastic film canister and lid
- an Alka-Seltzer tablet or generic effervescent stomach remedy
- safety goggles

CAUTION: AN ADULT ASSISTANT AND SAFETY GOGGLES ARE REQUIRED, BECAUSE THE CANISTER FLIES APART WITH CONSIDERABLE VELOCITY. DO THIS EXPERIMENT OUTSIDE AND AWAY FROM PEOPLE AND ANIMALS.

Pour water into an empty film canister until it is half full.

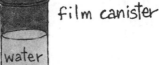

film canister

water

Break an Alka-Seltzer tablet in half. (Don't worry if the two pieces aren't equal.) Drop one of the halves into the film canister.

Drop half of an Alka-Seltzer tablet into the canister.

Quickly snap on the lid.

STAND BACK!

Quickly snap the lid on tightly and place the "bomb" on the ground. Move away six or seven feet.

Pow! The lid flies off, landing several yards from ground zero. This is so cool we're sure you won't let the other half of the Alka-Seltzer go to waste. You gotta try this again!

Insider Information

The propellant for this bomb is carbon dioxide gas, which is produced by a chemical reaction when the tablet and water mix. Alka-Seltzer contains baking soda and dehydrated citric acid. Both of these substances are necessary to produce the gas, but they won't react in a dry state. It is when you add water that the acid springs into action. This is the same reaction as mixing vinegar and baking soda. (See "A Plastic Explosion" on page 58.) We tried making a baking soda and vinegar bomb in the canister, but we couldn't get the lid on fast enough. Alka-Seltzer makes so much more gas that it doesn't matter if some escapes.

The chemical reaction produces a lot of gas in a closed space, and this creates pressure. The gas buildup breaks the container at its weakest point—the lid. You have created an IFO—an identifiable flying object.

FLAMELESS FIRE

Chemical hand warmers are the small packets of material that become hot after you rip open the outside wrappers and expose them to the air. They're just the right size to insert in your mittens and can keep your hands warm for five or six hours. You can buy inexpensive ones at many winter sports stores. But with our secret recipe, you won't have to. You can make them yourself.

You will need:
- 2 tablespoons iron powder (available from a machine shop, chemical supply house, or hobby shop)
- 2 tablespoons pulverized *activated* charcoal (available at pet stores; used for aquarium filters)
- 3 tablespoons fluffy, fine sawdust (usually available at your local lumberyard, or try the shavings from a pencil sharpener)
- 2 tablespoons vermiculite (available at garden stores or other places where plants are sold)
- 1 teaspoon salt

- 2 tablespoons water
- measuring spoons
- a sandwich-sized self-closing plastic bag

plastic bag

2 Tbsp. iron powder
2 Tbsp. activated charcoal
3 Tbsp. sawdust
2 Tbsp. vermiculite
1 Tsp. salt
2 Tbsp. water

*I*f you read the list of ingredients on the labels of commercial hand warmers, you'll see there is nothing exotic or magical in them. It may be a bit of a scavenger hunt to locate all the ingredients, but if you can't find exactly what you need, you can improvise. For instance, if you can get only coarse activated charcoal, put some in a plastic bag and smash it to a powder with a hammer.

Mix all the ingredients together in an open plastic bag. We didn't put air on the list, but it is absolutely necessary, so don't squeeze the bag tightly when you close the top. It takes only a few minutes for the heat to turn on. Your homemade hand warmer will generate heat for hours. Put the bag in your pocket. When it starts to cool, open the bag and shake the contents to add more air and then reseal it.

Insider Information

The heat comes from a chemical reaction when iron combines with oxygen to form rust. The same kind of reaction occurs when fuels burn, except that heat is given off rapidly enough to produce a flame. Rusting takes much longer. These reactions are called *exothermic*, because they emit heat.

Each ingredient has its own special role in the chemical reaction. The iron, of course, is the fuel. The salt and the activated charcoal speed up the process. The water brings the reacting materials together. The vermiculite holds and distributes the water evenly. The sawdust is an insulator that keeps the heat in.

Most of the heat is given off in the first few hours, although the reaction will continue until all the iron has rusted. This usually takes about twenty-four hours. Dead hand warmers, commercial and homemade alike, are environmentally friendly. They are nontoxic and biodegradable. You can feed the contents to an iron-loving azalea or holly plant.

A COOL REACTION

See a cool chemical combination.

If you tried "A Plastic Explosion"(page 58) or "A Gas Bomb"(page 62), you know that baking soda and acid react to produce carbon dioxide gas. You may not have noticed how *cool* this reaction really is.

You will need:
- water
- a liquid-measuring cup
- a digital meat thermometer
- measuring spoons
- vinegar
- baking soda
- a spoon

Pour about half a cup of warm water in the measuring cup. Take the temperature. One hundred to one hundred twenty degrees Fahrenheit works well. Leave the thermometer in the water. Add about two tablespoons of vinegar and a teaspoon of baking soda, then stir. Watch the thermometer as the bubbles form. When they stop, stir in another teaspoon of baking soda. Add another tablespoon of vinegar when the reaction dies down. Watch the temperature drop. We're such cool scientists that we got a twenty-degree drop in about one minute.

Insider Information

Some chemical reactions, like the one in "Flameless Fire" (page 65) or like fire itself, give off energy in the form of heat. Others use heat from the surroundings. They're called *endothermic* reactions. An example of this is the reaction between baking soda and an acid (vinegar).

Baking soda is a home remedy that relieves the burning of an upset stomach. It reacts with excess stomach acid and neutralizes it. In the process, it also lowers the body temperature, adding to the cooling effect of the medicine.

FLASHY FIRST AID

Create light with a strip bandage.

You don't need to wait until you're bleeding to produce light from a bandage. And you won't be wasting the bandage, either.

You will need:
- a Curad strip bandage (Don't use any other brand.)
- a room that is completely dark

Take a bandage into a dark room, and wait a few minutes for your eyes to become dark adapted. Keep your eyes on the bandage even though you can't see it. Grasp the wrapper tabs and quickly pull them apart. A flash of light comes from the wrapper. Exciting!

Insider Information

You're not the only excited thing. Believe it or not, the wrapper adhesive is also excited. That's what made the light. The glow is called *chemiluminescence.* When you pull the wrapper apart, you break the bonds between the adhesive molecules. The mechanical energy created by the ripping, compliments of you, is transferred to the adhesive molecules. Scientifically speaking, they are now in an excited state. As you know, excitement can't last forever, and the added energy is released as the molecules return to their resting state. This energy is released as light, which comes a split second after you've finished ripping open the wrapper.

Save the bandage by resealing the wrapper.

Claims have been made that you can see chemiluminescence with other adhesives. Try self-stick envelopes or electrical tape. The light flash can create enough heat under some circumstances to cause an explosion. A heavy-duty lead-acid battery that was being recharged in a restricted space once exploded when an operator peeled off some nearby electrical tape.

SECRET iNFoAMATiON

kill the head on root beer with a secret ingredient.

Some people like a large foamy head on their root beer, but if you're one of those who don't, there's an easy way to get rid of it.

> You will need:
> - milk or cream
> - root beer
> - 2 clear glasses
> - a friend

An odd bit of science trivia makes a mystifying magic trick. To set it up, place a drop of milk on the bottom of one of the glasses. No one is likely to notice it. Open a bottle of root beer and pour half of it into the other glass. Pour the soda from a height so a big head is formed. Hand the glass to a friend while saying, "I prefer mine without a head."

Pour the rest of the bottle into the doctored glass. Yours won't foam.

Insider Information

A foam is a mass of bubbles. Plain water and most sodas do not foam. In order to foam, a liquid must contain a dissolved substance that allows bubble walls to form. Unlike most sodas, root beer contains protein, which reinforces the bubble walls. When you open a bottle of root beer, releasing the pressure, carbon dioxide gas rushes to the surface, where tiny bubbles form and create a fairly long-lasting foam.

Milk contains fat molecules that interact with protein and prevent the bubbles from forming a stable foam.

A SQUARE EGG

Make a hard-boiled egg with corners.

Another word for *oval* is *egg-shaped*. There are definitely no square eggs in nature. So imagine how surprised your family and friends will be when you serve an egg shaped like an ice cube.

You will need:
- an extra-large egg
- a pot of water
- a stove
- cooking oil or spray

- a small plastic box about 1½ inches wide x 1½ inches long x 1½ inches high (We used a small square box designed to hold paper clips.)
- a spoon
- paper towels

CAUTION: BECAUSE THE ACTIVITY INVOLVES USING A STOVE, BOILING HOT WATER, AND HANDLING A VERY HOT HARD-BOILED EGG, DO THIS WITH AN ADULT ASSISTANT.

To square an egg, place it in a pot of cool water and bring the water to a boil. Let the water continue to boil rapidly for ten minutes. While the egg is cooking, grease the inside of the box with oil or cooking spray. Turn off the heat, and have your adult assistant remove the egg with a spoon. Do not throw out the water. Place the hot egg on several paper towels. Wrap the towels around the egg and gently tap the egg to crack the shell all over. Unwrap the egg and, bit by bit, carefully peel away the shell. Have your assistant occasionally dip the egg back into the hot water to wash off small pieces of shell and to keep the egg hot. When the shell has been removed, gently push the egg, pointed end first, into the plastic box. The egg should completely fill it. Put the lid on the box if it has one. Otherwise, weigh it down with a plate. Place the boxed egg in the refrigerator for at least a half hour.

The cooled egg should slide out of the box easily. But it has now been permanently altered into a distinctly unnatural shape.

Insider Information

Egg white is made of water and protein molecules that are like tiny balls of yarn. Cooking unravels the protein molecules and causes them to bond to one another. Water is trapped in the spaces between the protein molecules. The liquidy egg white now has the consistency of a gel, or flexible solid. While the gel is still hot, the protein bonds can be manipulated. They are flexible enough to be molded into a square shape. Additional bonds continue to form between protein molecules until the egg is cold. Then the shape becomes permanent.

ANT-ACID

Make ants use a chemical
weapon of destruction.

You can become a chemical weapons inspector.
Begin by monitoring the ant kingdom. Some of
these insects are able to release a colorless, smelly,
toxic acid that can blister human skin, corrode steel,
and melt plastics. You can detect it without any
danger to yourself with your trusty homemade acid-
indicator paper.

You will need:
- baking soda
- measuring spoons
- water
- a liquid-measuring cup
- a shallow pan larger than a sheet of
  paper
- Astrobrights Galaxy Gold paper
  (You can purchase this specific brand
  manufactured by Wausau Papers at
  many office supply stores, such as Office
  Max and Kinko's.)
- a few sheets of newspaper
- tweezers
- carpenter ants

77

First you have to make the paper. Dissolve one tablespoon of baking soda in a cup of water. Pour the solution into a shallow pan. Immerse a sheet of Astrobrights Galaxy Gold paper in the solution. It will turn bright red. Carefully lay the wet paper on the newspaper to dry. The red dye might stain, so handle it with caution.

When the paper is dry, you are ready to hunt for chemical weapons carriers. Take tweezers and the test paper outside. The most likely suspects are big black carpenter ants that make their home in rotten wood. When you have found a colony, gently pick up one of the ants with your tweezers and hold it over the test paper. Your tweezer attack will make the ant defend itself with a spray of powerful formic acid. Wherever a drop of formic acid hits, the paper will turn bright gold.

When you're finished, release the ant in the same place you found it.

Insider Information

Formic acid is the strongest acid produced by a living thing. One out of every ten ants in the world (that's 100 trillion) is a small formic acid factory. These ants use it as a defense against predators. People use it, too, in insecticides, food preservatives, textile and paper dyes, and disinfectants, among other things.

Ants make about 20 billion pounds of formic acid every year. However, we humans have not found a practical way to collect any quantity of it from ants. So industrial formic acid is produced synthetically, mainly from a waste product of paper mills.

BLOOD ON YOUR HANDS

Leave bloody fingerprints without actually bleeding.

You can fool your friends by leaving blood-red fingerprints on orange-gold paper. They'll think you've got blood on your hands, but they'll see that your hands are uninjured.

You will need:
- a sheet of Astrobrights Galaxy Gold paper (You can purchase this specific brand manufactured by Wausau Papers at many office supply stores, such as Office Max and Kinko's.)
- water
- baking soda

Prepare the blood bath by wetting a sheet of Astrobrights Galaxy Gold paper. Dip your dry fingers into baking soda. Wherever you touch your fingers to the wet paper, you will leave blood-red fingerprints.

Insider Information

Galaxy Gold was not designed to be a chemical test paper. But it is. The yellow dye turns red in the presence of chemicals that are *alkalis*, or *bases* (such as baking soda). It turns back to yellow when it comes in contact with chemicals that are *acids* (such as vinegar). The most famous acid-base test paper is litmus paper. Litmus is a natural dye that comes from lichens. The dye turns pink in acids and blue in bases.

If you're in a situation where you can't wet the paper, you can still leave a bloody mark. Dampen your fingers with a glass cleaner or household cleaner that includes ammonia. Then touch your wet fingers to the paper. Clearly the cleaner contains alkalis.

CODE RED

You've probably tried writing secret messages on paper with lemon juice or milk and developing them with heat. Use this high-tech spy paper and get much more colorful messages.

You will need:
- white vinegar
- measuring spoons
- water
- a liquid-measuring cup
- a paintbrush or cotton swab
- a sheet of Astrobrights Galaxy Gold paper (You can purchase this specific brand manufactured by Wausau Papers at many office supply stores, such as Office Max and Kinko's.)
- Windex
- a coconspirator

A dd a tablespoon of white vinegar to a half cup of water. Wet a paintbrush or cotton swab with the mixture, and write your coded message on a sheet of Astrobrights Galaxy Gold paper. Let the paper dry. When the paper is dry, your message will be invisible. It is now ready to be delivered.

To be read, your message has to be "developed." Instruct your fellow spy to lay the paper flat on a surface that is easily cleaned. Have him or her spray the paper evenly with Windex. The message stays yellow while the rest of the paper turns red. *This can be quite messy, so be careful not to get the red liquid on clothing or surfaces that could be damaged.*

Insider Information

In the previous experiment, "Blood on Your Hands," you discovered how Galaxy Gold paper can detect acids and bases. In this experiment, you wrote on the paper with acid (vinegar). Because the paper is already acidic, there was no color change.

Acids and bases neutralize each other. Windex, which is an alkali, neutralizes the acid in the yellow dye of the paper so that it changes to red. The writing contains extra acid from the vinegar. Therefore, extra Windex is needed to neutralize the message. If you want to erase your message completely, keep spraying with the Windex to neutralize the additional amount of acid—your "ink."

FREAKY FLUIDS

Fluids—gases and liquids—are shapeless. They flow from one place to another. That's normal. But fluids can take an unexpected direction and launch a tea bag into the air, create art in a glass of milk, or prevent you from drinking through a straw. Anyone can blow bubbles, but you will be able to create antibubbles.

Ordinary air and water can behave in freaky ways. You'll discover some of them in this chapter.

A REALLY BiG SUCKER

Suck through an extremely long straw.

Find out how big a sucker you are. Can you drink through a one-foot straw? A two footer? A five footer? If you're good, you may have to stand on a chair!

You will need:
- plastic straws
- scissors
- tape
- a beverage

To test your pucker power, make a maxistraw by joining plastic straws together. Because it is important that you get an airtight seal, make two half-inch slits in one end of each straw. Mesh the

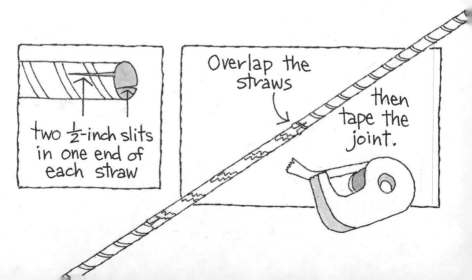

two ½-inch slits in one end of each straw

Overlap the straws

then tape the joint.

straws at the slits so that they overlap. Then tape the joint securely.

Start testing your lung power with a three-piece straw. Put it into your beverage and suck away. If you get a few good swallows, add another straw. Keep adding straws until you reach your limit. Vicki's last straw was number six. Kathy was not as big a sucker.

Insider Information

You suck a liquid up a straw by lowering the air pressure in your mouth. You aren't pulling up the liquid; it is being pushed up the straw by the greater pressure of the atmosphere pushing down on the liquid outside the straw.

There's a limit to the height water can rise. If there were a perfect vacuum above a column of water, that column would rise about thirty feet. You, however, are not a great vacuum pump. You can make only a partial vacuum in your mouth. In order to suck liquid through a three-foot straw, you must lower the atmospheric pressure in your mouth by one tenth. A six-foot straw means you've got to lower it to four-fifths of atmospheric pressure. Six feet is probably close to the maximum pressure reduction the human mouth and lungs can make.

BLOWING UP TOILET PAPER

A roll of toilet paper can become a flying streamer of immense proportions. All you need is a strong enough wind. A leaf blower is a homegrown hurricane. It produces a wind of 150 miles an hour, well into the hurricane range on the Beaufort scale.

You will need:
- a roll of toilet paper
- a broomstick
- a leaf blower
- a friend

Blowing up toilet paper requires two people. Go outside (that's where hurricanes belong, after all). Put the roll of toilet paper on a broomstick and hold the stick horizontally so that the toilet paper unrolls over the top. Unroll a few sheets and let them hang down. Now for the action. The person holding the leaf blower should aim the air stream so that it rushes over the top surface of the roll. The hanging t.p. rises, and the roll begins to unfurl, rapidly becoming an airborne banner.

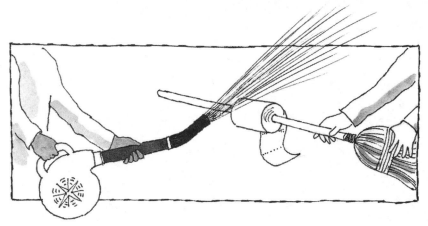

Insider Information
There are two things happening here: The toilet paper unrolls and the unraveling paper flies. It

unrolls because the enormous force of the airstream pushes against the top of the roll, making it spin. The unrolling paper takes off because the air passing over the top surface of the paper lowers the air pressure on that surface. The air pressure under the paper is now greater and the paper rises. The faster the air moves over the top surface, the smaller the downward pressure on that surface becomes. This is known as Bernoulli's principle, named for the Italian scientist who discovered it.

Bernoulli's principle explains how an airplane is able to stay up in the air. Plane wings are shaped so that air travels faster over the top surfaces. As long as the engine moves the plane forward, the air underneath the wings will lift up the plane.

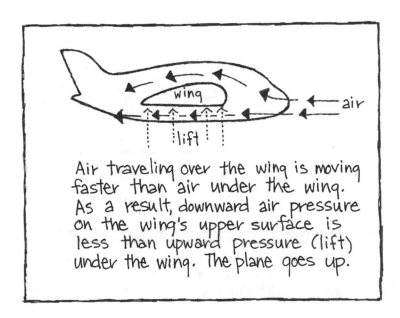

Air traveling over the wing is moving faster than air under the wing. As a result, downward air pressure on the wing's upper surface is less than upward pressure (lift) under the wing. The plane goes up.

THE FLYING TEA BAG

Burn a tea bag so it floats in the air.

If someone shows us a better mousetrap, we'll use it. A version of this trick appeared in our book *Bet You Can!* under the title "The Burning Question." You needed tissue paper, scissors, rubber cement, and a lot of fiddling to set it up. It's a lot simpler with a tea bag. So we're passing along this new twist, which came from Australia.

You will need:
- a Lipton flow-through tea bag
- a metal pie pan
- matches

> CAUTION: THIS INVOLVES FIRE, SO AN ADULT ASSISTANT IS REQUIRED.

Remove the staple from the tea bag. Unfold the bag and dump out the tea. (Since the Boston Tea Party, dumping tea has been an American tradition. You don't have to throw it away, however. Put it in a cup of hot water and drink it.) Use your fingers to open the paper so that it becomes a tube. Set the tube in the middle of the pie plate so it looks like a little chimney. Light a match and set fire to the top of the tube.

The tea-bag paper quickly burns from the top down. When the flame reaches the bottom, the ash-tube rises and floats in the air.

Insider Information

As the paper tube burns, a column of hot air forms inside it. Warm air rises. As cooler air rushes in to replace the rising column of warmer air, a *convection current* forms. This current of air is strong enough to lift the lightweight ash.

Lipton tea-bag paper works better than other types. First, it's already the right shape to make a column of hot air. Second, the special filter paper contains almost no additives such as the clay found in ordinary paper. Therefore, the ash left behind is extremely light.

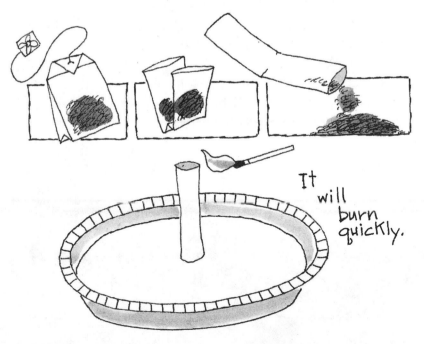

It will burn quickly.

THE SELF-PAINTING PICTURE

Make modern art in milk.

This art may not be to your taste, but it is not hard to swallow. Your canvas is white milk. Your paints are liquid food colors.

You will need:
- a glass of milk
- liquid food colors

Put a glass of milk on a counter or table and let it settle. It's important for the milk to remain still, so don't move the glass or shake the table while your picture is painting itself.

Put a drop of each color somewhere on the milk near the side of the glass. Wait. The colors will swirl and mix while you watch. This, however, is not art for eternity. If you wait too long, the colors blend completely and you'll have one yucky color. Better drink up while it still looks good.

Insider Information

Even when a liquid appears to be still, it is in motion. The molecules in milk and every other liquid are constantly moving. Food coloring is a highly concentrated substance. When food coloring and milk come in contact with each other, molecular motion causes them to mix without any outside help. No stirring or shaking is required. The self-mixing process is called *diffusion*.

During diffusion, molecules move from a crowded area (food coloring) to a less crowded area (milk). The path of the diffusion creates designs in the milk. Each glass of designer milk has a unique pattern. But the final result of all diffusion is the same: an even mixture of one color.

ANTiBUBBLES

Make liquid-filled bubbles.

An antibubble is not something we made up. It's similar to the kind of bubble you're familiar with— it's round and it breaks when you poke it. A regular bubble is a skin of water surrounding air; it can exist in either air or water. An antibubble is a globule of water surrounded by a skin of air; it exists only underwater.

You will need:
- a glass bowl or jar
- water
- measuring spoons
- liquid dishwashing detergent
- a glass measuring cup
- food coloring
- a clean, empty squeeze bottle with a hole about ⅛ inch in diameter (An Elmer's glue bottle, a contact lens solution bottle, or a ketchup or mustard squeeze bottle will do nicely.)
- salt (optional)
- honey or corn syrup (optional)

To make antibubbles, fill a bowl with water and at the same time squirt about a teaspoon of liquid dishwashing detergent into it. Keep a thin thread of water running into the bowl while you sweep off the foam at the top. Pour enough of the soap-and-water mixture into a measuring cup to fill the squeeze bottle. Add water to the bowl until it is almost full again. Then put a few drops of food coloring into the measuring cup, and stir gently. Fill the squeeze bottle with the colored liquid.

Squirt the bottle over the surface of the water in the bowl. Some of the colored liquid globules will skitter across the top of the water before they break, leaving a trail of color behind. Some globules will be pushed beneath the surface. These are your antibubbles.

antibubbles

It takes a bit of practice to create antibubbles. Experiment with different angles and try squirting with different pressures. A gentle squeeze seems to work best.

How can you spot an antibubble? Look for color or for bubbles that rise to the surface very slowly. With practice, you can produce a steady stream of antibubbles. We made particularly big ones by holding the squirt bottle vertically and placing one water globule directly on top of another.

Insider Information

An antibubble has a layer of liquid both inside and outside with a thin layer of air in between. A regular bubble has air inside and out with a thin layer of liquid in between. When you pop an antibubble, the liquid inside it joins the surrounding liquid, and the air layer forms a tiny regular bubble that quickly rises to the top. When you pop a regular bubble, the inside air joins the surrounding atmosphere and the liquid skin forms a tiny drop that falls to the ground.

In water, antibubbles, like air bubbles, rise to the surface. However, since antibubbles are mostly water with a very thin skin of air, they are just slightly lighter than the surrounding water. As a result, they take a much longer time to rise to the top than do air bubbles. If the fluid inside the antibubble is heavier than water, the bubble will actually sink. Salt water is heavier than regular water. So if you add salt to the water in your squeeze bottle, you can create some sinkers. When they hit the bottom of the bowl, they will break. If you want to prolong the life of your antibubbles, put a layer of honey or corn syrup on the bottom of the bowl to cushion the landing.

DiVING DUCK SAUCE

Sink packets of sauce without touching them.

Command packets of sauce to dive in a bottle of water. Amazingly, they not only obey you going down but also return to the surface when you tell them to.

> You will need:
> - duck sauce, soy sauce, ketchup, or other sauces in individual packets
> - a bowl of water
> - a clear plastic one-liter soda pop bottle with a screw top
> - water

Collect the candidates for your diving team the next time you're in a takeout or fast-food restaurant. Make sure the packets are unopened. Select your divers by putting the packets of sauce in a bowl of water. Choose the ones that are barely floating.

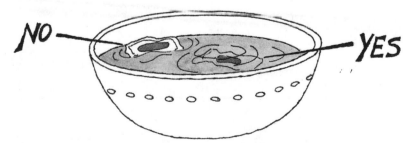

NO — YES

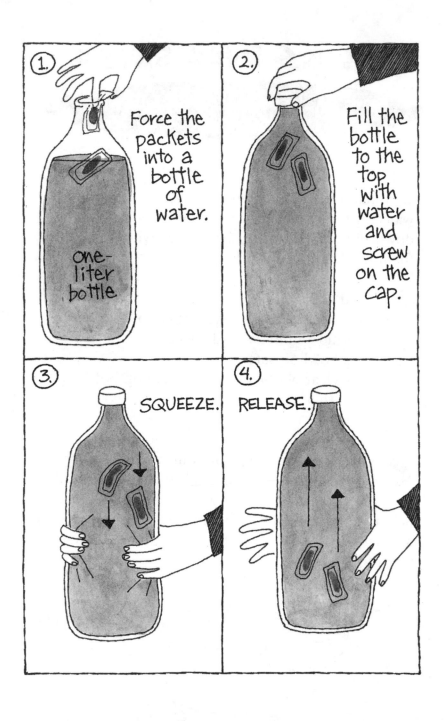

Prepare the diving chamber by removing the label from the one-liter bottle. Fill the bottle with water almost to the top. Force one or two packets of sauce through the opening. Add water until the bottle is filled completely. Screw on the top and you're ready.

Place your hands around the bottle and squeeze. The packets will head for the bottom if you've applied enough pressure. Release the pressure and they return to the surface. Once you have mastered the pressure regulation, you can even get the divers to stop halfway. When you entertain your friends, command the divers to "sink" or "swim." If you don't let them see you squeeze the bottle, the way your divers follow instructions will seem mysterious.

Insider Information

Just like fish, each of your divers has a swim bladder. The sauce packet contains a bubble of air that keeps it afloat. When you squeeze the bottle, the pressure on it is transmitted through the water, causing the bubble to shrink. The smaller bubble is less buoyant and the packet sinks. When you release the pressure, the bubble gets bigger and the packet floats. Fish change the size of the bubble in their swim bladder to regulate their depth.

It doesn't matter where you squeeze the bottle. The packets will dive because pressure to one part of the water in the bottle spreads evenly throughout all the water. This ability of a liquid to transmit pressure evenly has lots of practical applications. Hydraulic lifts in service stations and hydraulic brakes in cars are two examples.

ANTiBUBBLE GiZMo

Make this antibubble toy.

Once you have met the challenge of making anti-bubbles in water, try making them in other liquids. Endless numbers of antibubbles and waves are easily produced in this portable, perpetual antibubble gizmo.

You will need:
- a screw-top olive jar or any other tall, thin jar with the label removed
- vegetable oil
- rubbing alcohol
- food coloring

food coloring

rubbing alcohol

oil

our oil into the jar until it is half full. Then add rubbing alcohol until the jar is as full as it can be. Put in a drop or two of food coloring. Screw on the top. Check to make sure there are no air bubbles by turning the jar upside down. If there are bubbles, open the jar and add more rubbing alcohol. Test again. There must be no air bubbles.

Shake the jar and you will produce many patterns of antibubbles in the oil layer.

Insider Information

You've produced a different kind of antibubble in your gizmo. Because the jar is full, there is no air present, so you can only produce a "liquid in a liquid" bubble. The food coloring detects the presence of rubbing alcohol, which forms the skin.

The antibubble gizmo has no known practical value. However, staring at it has a mysterious soothing effect. Just be sure you don't leave it where it might be mistaken for a soft drink.

REALLY WEIRD STUFF 5

There's a branch of science devoted to discovering the properties of materials. Once scientists know what stuff is like, engineers can figure out useful things to do with it or—as in this chapter—some useless but entertaining applications. Causing a coin to appear to pass through a solid and making tonic water glow are only two of the "apps" you've just gotta try.

SLICK TRICK

Stack ice cubes to see how easily success can slip away.

You're not going to build an ice castle. The object of this slick trick is just to pile ice cubes one on top of another. Good luck! Ice cubes are not bricks. They slip off each other as the tower grows.

You will need:
- ice cubes
- a plate
- table salt

There is a way to build a cool tower (more than three cubes high). Before you try stacking the ice cubes, let them sit on a plate at room temperature for two or three minutes. Then generously

sprinkle salt on the top surface of each cube before putting another one on top of it. Practice stacking and you may beat our record of five cubes.

Insider Information

There are two reasons why the ice cubes don't slip in your salted stack. First, salt lowers the freezing point of water. The ice melts around each grain of salt as the salt dissolves. As a result, the ice is unevenly eaten away, forming a pitted, nonskid surface. (This is why salt is used to melt ice on roads and walkways.)

Second, the water, now salted, refreezes on the surface of the ice cubes, joining them together. This happens because the insides of the ice cubes are much colder than the freezing point of water. They are cold enough to draw heat out of the newly melted water, and it refreezes.

TWISTED THOUGHTS

Make a self-twisting rope.

Twist a piece of string and let it go. The twist untwists. Always. Well, not always. Rope is permanently twisted string. It's not hard to make if you know the trick. Rope literally makes itself.

You will need:
- 3 twenty-four-inch lengths of string or yarn
- a chair
- scissors

To make a rope, tie three pieces of string to a chair. Twist one strand in a clockwise direction until it is tightly wound. Don't let go—you know what will happen if you do! So, while holding on to your twisted string, twist the other strings in the same clockwise direction, one at a time. Then stretch out the three twisted lengths of string and let go of the ends. Ta da! A rope forms before your very eyes. Now cut it off the chair. Don't worry—the ends will not unravel.

Insider Information

When you let go and the strings untwist, they wrap around the strands next to them. This keeps them from untwisting completely.

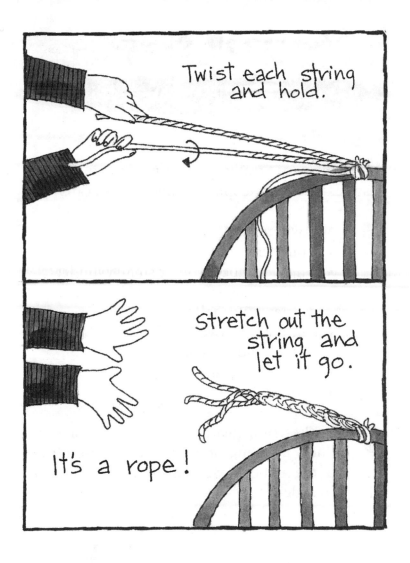

Ropes are twisted both to keep them from unraveling and to increase their strength. Tiny fibers are twisted to make thread; threads are twisted to make stronger strings; strings are twisted to make even stronger rope.

DROP SHOT

Pass a coin through a solid.

Okay, you're not really going to pass a coin through a solid. However, people will believe you can.

You will need:
- a quarter
- a lipstick tube or other small cylinder with a diameter about the size of a quarter, but smaller
- a thin latex glove (the kind used by doctors and dentists)
- a small clear jar
- a rubber band

Place the coin, heads up, on top of a small cylinder standing on a tabletop. Rinse off the inside of the rubber glove to get rid of its coating of talcum powder.

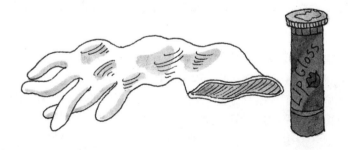

Stretch the palm part of the glove over the coin by pulling down evenly in all directions. Stretch the latex thin enough so that the image on the coin is clearly visible. Now ease off the pressure. The latex will trap the coin, and it will appear to be sitting on the top surface of the latex. Warning: Don't pull too hard or the rubber will tear.

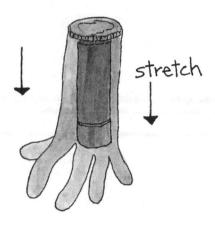

stretch

Stretch the glove gently over the mouth of a small jar, being careful not to dislodge the coin. Fasten the glove with a rubber band. The coin, which is really on the underside of the rubber, looks as if it is sitting on top of it.

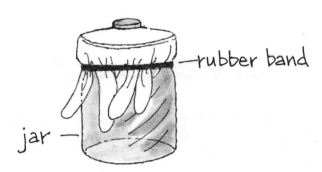

rubber band

jar

Once you're set up, invite an audience. Claim that you can make the coin pass through the latex without making a hole in it. Follow up by giving the coin a tap from above. It will drop like a shot into the jar, leaving the rubber undamaged.

Insider Information

Latex rubber is a material that has a memory. You can bend it or stretch it, but when the distorting force is removed, the rubber returns to its original shape. You're exploiting this property twice in this trick. The round shape of the coin is a key element in trapping it in the rubber. When the rubber is stretched over the rim of the coin and then released, the latex underneath the coin pulls together to form a ring that holds the coin in place.

When you release the coin with your tap, the latex that was underneath the coin is then free to return to its original flat, unstretched state.

Insider Information

Pure ultraviolet light is invisible to the human eye. It's just below our threshold of vision. You can see the glow of an ultraviolet lightbulb because its rays aren't purely ultraviolet. Some longer, visible, violet wavelengths are also emitted by the bulb.

Quinine, the bitter-tasting ingredient in tonic water, is what makes the liquid glow. When ultraviolet light strikes quinine molecules, they absorb its energy, becoming excited. This excited state isn't permanent, however. Almost immediately, the quinine molecules lose the extra energy—but as visible light. This process, where uv light is transformed into visible light, is called *fluorescence*. The glow of a fluorescent lightbulb is caused by uv light striking a fluorescent coating on the inside of the bulb.

EXCiTiNG SODA

Tonic water may not excite you—but you can excite it!

You will need:
- tonic water
- a glass
- an ultraviolet (uv) light (available at a party store or a lighting store)

Take some tonic water and a glass into a dark room. Shine an ultraviolet, or "black," light on the tonic water while you pour it into the glass.

Under ordinary light, tonic water is a clear, bubbly liquid. Under uv light, it is transformed into an eerie, luminous fluid with a fluorescent blue glow.

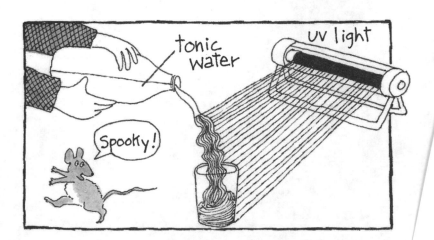

Some Other Really Cool Fluorescent Things You Gotta Try

- the Mylar strip on a new $100 bill
- a parakeet's feathers
- certain kinds of flowers (Bees can see uv light. Some flowers have uv patterns to guide the insects to their pollen.)
- laundry detergent with whiteners added
- various white or Day-Glo papers
- colored chalks (Many are made with crushed fluorescent minerals.)

A CLEAN CUT

Make a saw from kitchen cleanser.

Criminals in New York City once used an unusual saw to break out of jail. With only cotton string and powdered kitchen cleanser, they cut right through the iron bars of their cell. You too can create this innovative tool.

You will need:
- powdered kitchen cleanser
- water
- a two-foot length of cotton string
- a clamp
- a small piece of wood, such as a pencil

Sprinkle cleanser in the sink. Add a little water to make a thick paste. Rub the string in the paste until it is wet and caked with the cleanser. Straighten out the coated string and let it dry.

When the string is dry, clamp a pencil to a counter or have a friend hold it steady. Hold a section of the string tightly between your hands. Rub the string saw back and forth across the pencil. Move to a new section of the string when the old one stops cutting.

string caked with cleanser

pencil

Insider Information

Kitchen cleanser contains an abrasive substance. By embedding it in string, you give the string a cutting surface. Because the abrasive is fine, the cuts are tiny. It takes hundreds of them to saw a pencil in two. It also takes time. It took us about four minutes to cut through a pencil, so imagine how long it took to cut through iron bars!

EXCITING TV

See an image on a TV that's turned off.

Tonic water is not the only thing around the house that can get excited. TVs are very excitable, too.

You will need:
- a TV set
- a strong flashlight

You must do this experiment in a dark room with the TV turned off. Hold the flashlight in one hand. Place your other hand flat against the TV screen. Turn on the flashlight and shine the light all over the screen. Do this for at least two minutes, making sure that all of the screen is illuminated.

Turn off the flashlight and take away your hand. You will see a dark image of your hand on a glowing screen. It will be visible for a few minutes.

You can also use your TV screen as a notepad. Put the lit flashlight against the screen, write with the light, and then extinguish it. Enjoy the luminous message you've left behind.

Insider Information

A TV picture is created by a beam of electrons that scans back and forth across the screen from top to bottom about sixty times a second. The back of the screen is coated with a material that becomes excited with extra energy when struck by electrons. The light from a flashlight can also excite this screen coating material. In each case, the material absorbs energy and reemits it as a glowing light.

This phenomenon, called *phosphorescence*, is similar to the fluorescence you observed in "Exciting Soda" (page 113). There are, however, two big differences. First, phosphorescent material becomes excited when it is struck by *visible* light as opposed to ultraviolet light. And second, a phosphorescent glow continues for a few seconds after the light source has been turned off. This differs from a fluorescent glow, which disappears as soon as the uv light stops shining.

The black silhouette of your hand is visible because your hand kept the light from hitting the phosphorescent strips underneath it. Instead of a hole in the ozone, you've made a hole in the glow zone.

BOLT FROM THE BALLOON

Light a fluorescent lightbulb with a balloon.

How many balloons does it take to light a fluorescent lightbulb? This isn't a joke! You *can* light a bulb with a balloon—and it only takes one.

You will need:
- safety glasses
- a fluorescent lightbulb
- an inflated balloon
- a piece of wool or fur

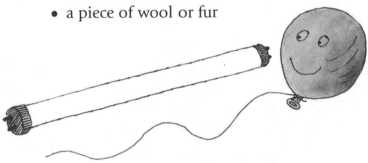

CAUTION: BE CAREFUL WHEN HANDLING FLUORESCENT LIGHTBULBS. THEY MIGHT EXPLODE IF BROKEN. DO THIS EXPERIMENT WITH AN ADULT ASSISTANT, AND WEAR PROTECTIVE GLASSES.

Rub the balloon on fur to give it a charge of static electricity.

Bring your equipment and your assistant into a darkened room. Have the assistant hold the lightbulb. Give the balloon a charge of static electricity by rubbing it repeatedly with a piece of wool or fur. (The length of time you need to rub will vary, depending on how humid the air is.) A charged balloon will make the hair on your arm stand on end.

Touch the charged balloon to the prongs at the end of the bulb. Flashes of light will briefly pulse up and down the tube. This may not work if the humidity is high. If you're not successful, try again on a dry day.

Touch the balloon to the end of the bulb.

Insider Information

Surprise. It doesn't take much energy to light a fluorescent bulb. That's why these bulbs are so cheap to run.

A fluorescent light is a hollow glass tube painted on the inside with a fluorescent material. Some of the air has been pumped out of the tube and replaced with mercury vapor. When the light is turned on, electricity flows from one end of the tube to the other. The electrons strike the mercury atoms, which become briefly excited. When the atoms return to their unexcited state, they release the extra energy as ultraviolet light. The uv light hits the fluorescent paint, where it is converted into visible light.

When you rub a balloon, you give it a negative charge, because it picks up an excess of electrons from the fur. These electrons jump to the metal end of the bulb when you bring the balloon close. This is enough energy to produce a brief flash of fluorescent light.

Excess electrons jump to the metal end of the bulb.

COUNTERFEIT MONEY DETECTOR

Identify bogus bills with iodine.

The U.S. government tries to make money that is difficult to counterfeit. Perfect replicas of the design are easy to make with a hi-tech color copier, but it's impossible for counterfeiters to duplicate the special paper.

CAUTION: IODINE IS A POISON. USE EXTREME CARE NOT TO GET IT IN YOUR EYES OR MOUTH. HAVE AN ADULT PRESENT WHEN YOU DO THIS TEST. ALSO, BE CAREFUL NOT TO GET IODINE ON YOUR CLOTHES OR SKIN, AS IT LEAVES STAINS THAT CANNOT BE REMOVED EASILY.

You will need:
- a cotton swab
- iodine
- American paper currency
- an assortment of other paper

Your medicine cabinet is the source of a test that quickly identifies most fake bills. Dip a cotton swab in the iodine. Touch it to paper money. The iodine will make a dull orange mark if the money is

genuine. It will turn black on fake money and on other kinds of paper.

Insider Information

Iodine turns black in the presence of a starch. Most paper contains starch, which adds bulk and holds the wood fibers together. The paper used for U.S. currency is made mostly of linen fibers, which cling together without any starch.

People who handle large amounts of cash are always on the lookout for counterfeits. To detect bogus money, they mark suspect bills with a special pen that contains iodine ink. These pens can be purchased at office supply stores.

Money is being redesigned with many new safeguards to make a counterfeiter's life miserable. The paper used in $20 bills and larger denominations is now manufactured with an embedded Mylar strip that has the value of the bill printed on it. In new $100 bills, this strip is fluorescent and glows under ultraviolet light.

NUKE KNACKS

The original use of microwaves was for military purposes: Radar detects enemy craft with microwaves. When a radar engineer discovered a melted candy bar in his pocket, he realized that microwaves could be used to heat food. His company then produced the first microwave ovens, called Radaranges.

Microwaves are an invisible form of light energy, or electromagnetic radiation. In an oven, penetrating microwaves cause the water molecules in food and other materials to vibrate. And a vibrating molecule is a hot molecule. The other chapters in this book have some really cool stuff. But we know that this one has the hottest tricks of all.

CAUTION: MICROWAVE OVENS PRODUCE HEAT. THE EXPERIMENTS IN THIS CHAPTER *MUST* BE DONE WITH ADULT HELP. HAVE POT HOLDERS HANDY, AND USE THEM WHENEVER YOU HANDLE HOT DISHES. AND DON'T LEAVE YOUR EXPERIMENT UNATTENDED IN THE MICROWAVE. NOT ONLY WILL YOU MISS THE FUN, BUT ALSO YOU NEED TO BE READY TO SHUT OFF THE OVEN IN CASE OF AN EMERGENCY. IF A FIRE SHOULD OCCUR IN THE MICROWAVE OVEN, LEAVE THE DOOR CLOSED AND TURN OFF OR UNPLUG THE OVEN.

MAP YOUR MICROWAVE

Nuke fax paper.

Some spots in a microwave get hotter than others. That's why manufacturers recommend that you rotate food during cooking. Want to know the best place to put your food? Fax the answer to yourself.

> You will need:
> - a piece of thermal fax paper
> - scissors
> - a microwave oven
> - a marker

Get a piece of thermal fax paper from a fax machine. Put a small mark on the shinier side, the side facing up as it comes from the machine. This is the only side that is heat sensitive. Cut the paper to fit the bottom of your microwave. Place it in the oven with the marked side up. Nuke on high for about seven minutes.

thermal fax paper

You now have a thermal map of your microwave. The hottest spots are the darkest; the cooler areas are white.

Insider Information

Microwaves are really waves. Like water waves, they bounce off surfaces such as the oven walls. When a bouncing wave encounters an incoming wave, they combine to form a larger wave called a *standing wave*. Standing waves stay in the same place. In a microwave oven, the standing waves form hot spots. Each microwave oven has its own pattern of hot spots. You've mapped your oven floor, but if you place the paper above the level of the floor, you may get a different pattern.

Learn where to put your food so it cooks the fastest!

ERUPTING SOAP

Transform an ordinary bar of Ivory soap into an erupting volcano of foam!

This theatrical effect does not work with ordinary soaps. Only air-filled Ivory puts on a show.

> You will need:
> - a regular-size bar of Ivory soap
> - a paper plate
> - a microwave oven

Begin your experiment into the world of slow motion explosions by unwrapping a regular-size bar of Ivory soap. Place the soap on a paper plate in a microwave oven, preferably one with a glass door so that you can watch the eruption.

Nuke the soap for two minutes on full power. Your previously firm bar of soap is now a light and fluffy mound of frothy, expanded soap foam.

Insider Information

Your soap eruption is courtesy of two industrial accidents.

The first was the discovery of the heating properties of microwaves.

The second accident created Ivory soap. A

machine that mixed soap was inadvertently left on during lunch. When the machine operator returned, he found that the overly mixed batch of soap had had air beaten into it. The resulting soap floated. People liked the floating soap, and the mistake turned into a marketing success.

How do two accidents equal one volcano? Ivory, like all soap, contains water. Microwaves cause water molecules to vibrate. The faster they vibrate, the hotter the water gets. When they vibrate fast enough, the water molecules turn into steam. Unlike other soaps, Ivory is honeycombed with thin-walled air spaces. The pressure of the steam breaks down the walls of the air spaces, and a big puff ball of soap grows until all the steam has escaped.

This experiment will not harm your microwave oven, although it does tend to make your kitchen smell like a laundry. Speaking of laundry, your soap volcano doesn't have to go to waste. Press the puff ball, and ta da—Ivory flakes that you can use for washing. You have made a significant discovery in the field of good clean fun!

MONSTER MARSHMALLOW

Toast a marshmallow from the inside out!

Picture a toasted marshmallow. Black and brown on the outside, white and gooey on the inside. Toasting a marshmallow in a microwave oven is a totally different experience.

> You will need:
> - a marshmallow
> - a paper plate
> - a microwave oven

Put a marshmallow on a paper plate and nuke it. The length of time will depend on the strength of your microwave oven. (Ours took one minute and thirty seconds on high.) As the microwaves bombard the marshmallow, it appears to become a living thing: It grows to three times its original size, and it moves and sways.

Remove the paper plate from the oven. *But don't touch the monster marshmallow—it's very hot.* Give it a few minutes to cool. Watch as it slowly shrinks and shrivels. The outside is white and looks uncooked. Break it open. The inside is brown. You've toasted your marshmallow from the inside out!

Eat your experiment when it's cool. It is crunchy and delicious.

Insider Information

Microwave ovens cook by making water molecules in the food vibrate. The faster the molecules vibrate, the hotter the food gets. When the water gets hot enough, it changes into steam and escapes. This causes the tiny air spaces in the marshmallow to expand.

Unlike a campfire, which cooks from the outside in, microwaves penetrate the marshmallow and cook it all at once. The inside temperature of the marshmallow gets hot enough to brown the sugar. The outside surface is cooled by escaping steam. Evaporation always produces a cooling effect, so the surface doesn't get hot enough to turn brown. The marshmallow will become brown and burn after all the steam has escaped, so be careful to turn off the microwave oven as soon as the puffing has stopped.

FiREWORKS FROM A GRAPE

Nuke a grape.

Would you believe pyrotechnics from a grape?

You will need:
- a green seedless grape
- a table knife
- a microwave-safe plate
- a microwave oven

To prepare a grape for this heat-and-light show, carefully slice it almost in half, leaving the halves attached by skin. Place the grape on a microwave-safe plate with the cut sides down. Put the plate in the center of a microwave oven. Nuke it on high for thirty seconds. Watch it through the door.

Slice the grape ...

... but leave the halves attached by skin.

Within five seconds, sparks shoot between the grape halves. Three to four seconds later, lightning arcs over the skin bridge, and the force blasts the two halves of the grape apart, ending the show. At this point, turn off the microwave to prevent any damage to the oven or further damage to the grape.

Insider Information

There isn't a simple explanation for the grape explosion, but this is what some of the best minds around think happens. 1. Grape juice conducts electricity. 2. Microwaves not only heat the water in the grape but also force a small amount of electricity coming from the grape back and forth through the skin bridge. This heats the bridge hot enough for it to catch on fire. 3. The microwaves begin to pass through the flame, which can also conduct electricity. This kind of electric current forms a brilliant light arcing back and forth between the grape halves. By the time this happens, the bridge has been burned, so to speak. 4. The arcing current is strong enough to blast the grape halves apart.

Not bad for a fruit that's just one of the bunch.

SUPERHEATED WATER

Use sugar to make water boil.

How can you tell when water is boiling? Easy—look for the bubbles rapidly rising to the surface of the pot. But boiling water in a microwave oven is different. It can be boiling hot without a bubble in sight!

You will need:
- a one-cup Pyrex measuring cup
- water
- a teaspoon
- sugar
- a microwave oven
- a pot holder

CAUTION: SINCE THIS TRICK INVOLVES NOT ONLY A MICROWAVE OVEN BUT ALSO BOILING HOT WATER, AN ADULT ASSISTANT IS DEFINITELY REQUIRED.

Put water in a Pyrex measuring cup and place it in the microwave oven. Nuke the water on high for two minutes and thirty seconds. The water is now hot enough to boil.

Have your adult assistant remove the cup from

the oven, using a pot holder if necessary. Place the cup on a heat-resistant surface. Sprinkle a teaspoon of sugar across the surface. Within seconds, a rush of tiny bubbles foams over the surface of the water.

Insider Information

Water boils when water molecules move fast enough to escape from the liquid into the air as steam. When you boil water in a pot on the stove, the water is heated from the bottom up. The hottest water molecules join together to form bubbles of steam on the bottom of the pot. Then the bubbles break loose and rise to the top.

In a microwave oven, all the water in the cup is heated at the same time but not evenly. (Remember those hot spots in your oven.) Although some molecules are moving fast enough to escape, they can be trapped by slower-moving surrounding molecules, which prevent them from getting together to form a bubble. The sharp edges of the sugar crystals have tiny points that disturb the hot liquid and allow the fast-moving molecules to get together and form bubbles.

iNSiDE JOB

Blow up a balloon inside a bottle.

It's not possible for a person to inflate a balloon inside a bottle using lung power. However, you can do it with steam power.

> CAUTION: THIS EXPERIMENT INVOLVES STEAM. WITH PROPER ADULT SUPERVISION, IT IS PERFECTLY SAFE. BUT DO *NOT* ATTEMPT THE EXPERIMENT WITHOUT AN ADULT PRESENT. OF COURSE AN ADULT SHOULD BE PRESENT ANYWAY, BECAUSE YOU ARE USING A MICROWAVE.

You will need:
- a tablespoon
- water
- an empty twelve-ounce glass bottle with the label removed
- a microwave oven
- oven mitts
- a small balloon

Put a tablespoon of water into a clear glass bottle. *Do not use a plastic bottle. It will melt in the microwave.* Place the uncapped bottle in a microwave oven. (If your microwave is too small, turn the bottle on its side.) Nuke it on high. Set the timer for three minutes, but watch the bottle through the window. Stop the oven when the water is *almost* boiled away. At this point, the bottle is very hot and full of steam.

Stop when the water is almost boiled away.

Have your adult assistant *use oven mitts* to remove the bottle and set it on a heat-resistant surface. Be careful not to knock the bottle over.

Have your helper place the hot bottle on a heat-resistant surface.

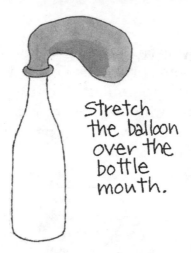

Stretch
the balloon
over the
bottle
mouth.

Your assistant should then take off the oven mitts and immediately stretch the neck of the balloon over the mouth of the bottle.

Watch as the bottle cools. The balloon will be sucked into the bottle and will inflate until it fills the interior.

The two of you have now created a mysterious object. See if anyone can figure out how it was made.

Insider Information

The microwave oven heats the water so that it boils and changes into steam. The steam drives out all the air in the bottle. If you had left the bottle alone, the steam would have cooled and condensed back into a very small amount of water. Air would have pushed into the bottle to replace the space left by the condensing steam. Since you put a balloon over the bottle while it was full of steam, the returning air pushed against the balloon, inflating it inside the bottle.

You got around one impossibility only to create another: Bet you can't remove the balloon without breaking the seal.

Index